Timber!
A Tale in Which a Son Learns to Honor His Parents

May you honor your parents so it may go well with you in the land! Christ's joy, J. Reneé Johnson

by J. Reneé Johnson
illustrated by Laura Nienhaus Zarrin

In Celebration™, Grand Rapids, MI

Library of Congress Cataloging-in-Publication Data

Johnson, J. Reneé (Julie Reneé), 1973-
    Timber! : a tale in which a son learns to honor his parents / by J. Reneé Johnson ;
illustrated by Laura Nienhaus Zarrin.
        p. cm. -- (Stories to grow by)
    Summary: Billy B. thinks he knows all about cutting timber, so when he goes out to the
woods with his father for the first time, he decides not to follow all the rules. Includes a
Bible verse and facts about beavers.
    ISBN 1-56822-593-8 (hardcover)
    [1. Beavers--Fiction. 2. Obedience--Fiction. 3. Fathers and sons--Fiction. 4. Christian
life--Fiction.] I. Zarrinnaal, Laura Nienhaus, ill. II. Title. III. Series.

PZ7.J63227 Ti 2000
[E]--dc21
                                                                    00-022236

Credits
Author: J. Reneé Johnson
Cover and Inside Illustrations: Laura Nienhaus Zarrin
Project Director/Editor: Alyson Kieda

ISBN: 1-56822-593-8
Timber!
Copyright © 1999 by In Celebration®
a division of Instructional Fair Group, Inc.
a Tribune Education Company
3195 Wilson Drive NW
Grand Rapids, Michigan 49544

For information regarding permission write to:
In Celebration®, P.O. Box 1650, Grand Rapids, MI 49501.

Printed in Singapore

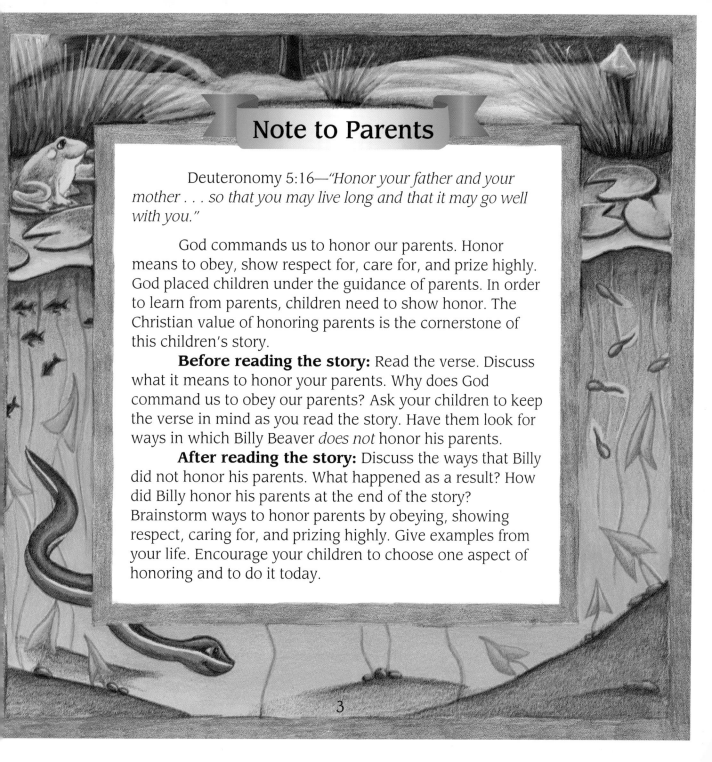

Note to Parents

Deuteronomy 5:16—*"Honor your father and your mother . . . so that you may live long and that it may go well with you."*

God commands us to honor our parents. Honor means to obey, show respect for, care for, and prize highly. God placed children under the guidance of parents. In order to learn from parents, children need to show honor. The Christian value of honoring parents is the cornerstone of this children's story.

Before reading the story: Read the verse. Discuss what it means to honor your parents. Why does God command us to obey our parents? Ask your children to keep the verse in mind as you read the story. Have them look for ways in which Billy Beaver *does not* honor his parents.

After reading the story: Discuss the ways that Billy did not honor his parents. What happened as a result? How did Billy honor his parents at the end of the story? Brainstorm ways to honor parents by obeying, showing respect, caring for, and prizing highly. Give examples from your life. Encourage your children to choose one aspect of honoring and to do it today.

In the cozy, round-roofed lodge, Mama B set bowls of willow twigs on the table. Then she sighed. "That Billy!" she said to Papa B. "I've called him for breakfast three times. The sun is going down and he's still not ready!"

Papa B picked up a twig and chuckled. "It's a big night when a beaver goes out for the first time to cut timber. I remember the first time I went out to the woods with my father. I was so excited I couldn't eat a thing."

Just then, Billy Beaver waddled into the room and slapped his tail on the floor excitedly. "Are you ready to go, Papa B? I am!" His eyes sparkled beneath his bright red Timber School hat.

"Son, you need to eat a big breakfast," said Mama B.
"And you'll have to leave that hat at home," said Papa B.
"It might attract a bear."
Billy's head drooped. "But, Papa B, it's my lucky hat!
A bear won't see it in the dark. Please . . ."

Mama B set a plate of twigs and
bark in front of Billy and chided gently,
"Billy, you need to listen to your father.
Timber cutting must be done just so.
Papa B has been doing it for years.
He knows what's safe and what isn't."

6

Billy looked pleadingly at Papa B, who finally nodded and said, "All right, son. You can wear the hat—but just for tonight, understand?"

Billy jumped down from the table. "I understand, Papa B! It's time to go! Let's get to work!"

Mama B shook her head worriedly. Papa B gave her a quick hug and said, "All right, Billy. Let's get going."

The two beavers dove into their lodge tunnel and swam underwater, surfacing in the rushing river. It was a beautiful night with a full moon and a sky full of sparkling stars. Even the wind seemed to whisper happily. Billy said to himself, "This is great! I'm going to show Papa B everything I learned at Timber School!"

When they reached the timber site, the beavers shook the water out of their silky fur. Billy started to run ahead, but Papa B grabbed quickly onto his tail. "Whoa, there!" Papa B said. "Before we begin, there are some important rules you need to know."

8

Billy danced with impatience. "Papa B, I know, I know! I just finished school, remember? I know everything about cutting timber!"

Papa B held back a fond smile. "Everything? That's a lot for a beaver to know. All right then, Billy. Tell me the two most important rules."

"Always listen for bears," said Billy promptly. "Because when a tree falls, it makes a noise that tells the bears we're here."

"Very good," said Papa B. "What else?"

Billy hopped up and down with excitement. "Well, at school they told us that when a tree is ready to fall, we shout 'Timber!' and then dive into the water where it's safe."

Papa B nodded. "That's right, Billy, because you never know which way the tree will fall."

Billy grinned from ear to ear. "But, Papa B, guess what? I can! I always know which way the tree will fall! Even my teacher said I was right every time! So I don't have to dive into the water. I can stay and watch my trees come down!"

10

Papa B looked stern. "Billy, no one can be right every time about a tree. The wind can shift, or die down, and the tree might fall on top of you. Besides, a nearby bear might come running faster than you think. I forbid you to stay on the shore."

"But, Papa B . . . I wanted to show you how good I am at this!" said Billy, his voice trembling with disappointment.

"Promise me," said Papa B, still stern.

"All right," Billy mumbled. But he crossed two of his toes. I've waited too long for this night to have it spoiled by Papa B's rules, he thought.

"No tree will fall on me," he whispered to himself. "I'm smart enough to know which way the tree will fall!"

In the white moonlight, Papa B led Billy to the two aspens that he wanted to haul back to the lodge. Billy gnawed into the bitter wood of his tree as fast as he could, but Papa B was even faster. Before Billy could finish his tree, Papa B called out, "Billy, head for the river! Timber!"

As he waddled quickly to the shore, Billy looked back over his shoulder. "I bet that tree will fall toward the shore," he thought. Then he dove into the river next to Papa B.

Moments later, a loud CRRRR-ACK pierced the darkness. When Billy heard the tree topple, he bobbed up to see if he had been right. But Papa B held him back. "Just a minute, Billy. We need to wait and see if a bear will show up." Billy sighed. After what seemed like an hour, Papa B said, "All clear."

Billy hopped onto the sandy shore and saw that Papa B's tree lay with its branches stretching to the water. "I was right!" he thought. "Right again!"

13

Papa B began to gnaw and tear branches off the fallen tree, while Billy hurried over to topple his. When the tree started to wobble on its trunk, Billy shouted, "Timber, Papa B! Timber!"

"It will fall back toward the woods," thought Billy as he heard Papa B splash into the water. "It's my very first tree. It won't hurt to watch just this once."

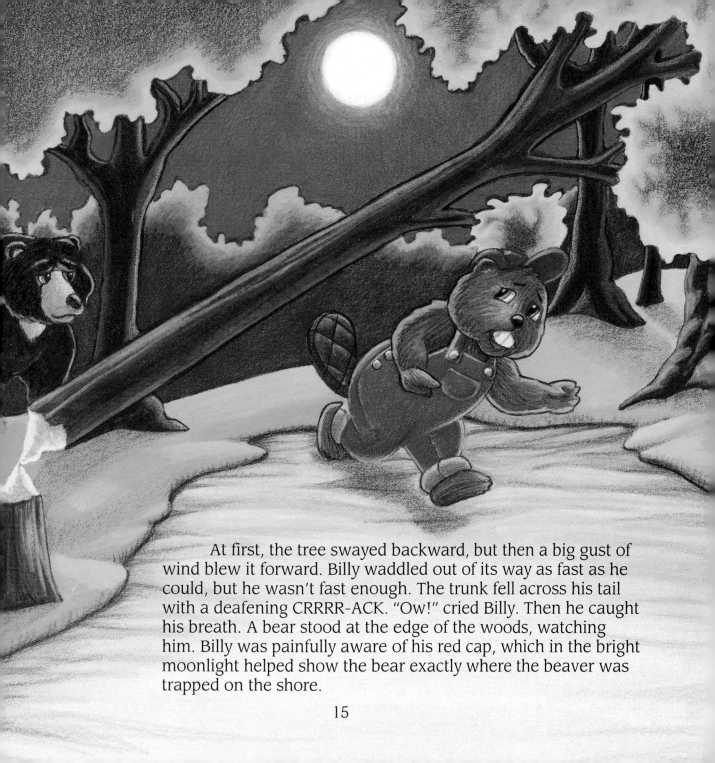

At first, the tree swayed backward, but then a big gust of wind blew it forward. Billy waddled out of its way as fast as he could, but he wasn't fast enough. The trunk fell across his tail with a deafening CRRRR-ACK. "Ow!" cried Billy. Then he caught his breath. A bear stood at the edge of the woods, watching him. Billy was painfully aware of his red cap, which in the bright moonlight helped show the bear exactly where the beaver was trapped on the shore.

Billy tugged and pulled, but his tail wouldn't budge. The bear lumbered slowly toward him. Suddenly, Billy felt a firm grip on his paw. It was Papa B.

"Hold on, son," whispered Papa B. There was no time to dig under the aspen to free Billy's tail. Papa B pulled as hard as he could. Billy's tail yanked free and the two beavers fell head over heels into the water. The bear growled and charged.

16

"Swim, Billy!"
yelled Papa B.
    Papa B pulled Billy into
deeper water as the bear splashed
into the shallows toward them. Then the
beavers dove underwater and swam all the
way to the lodge tunnel and safety.

17

Later, after they were safe in the lodge, Billy blurted out, "I'm sorry, Papa B. You were right. I nearly got us killed."

"Well," said his father, leaning back in his chair, "I seem to remember another young beaver that made some big mistakes, too."

"You mean you, Papa B?"

Papa B nodded. "I learned, though. I found that if I listened to my father, his rules kept me safe. And they still do, to this day."

"Sounds like we come from a long line of smart timber-cutters," said Billy.

Papa B smiled. "And you'll be one of them, son."

A Note About Beavers

Beavers are furry animals with wide, flat tails that resemble paddles. Beavers are skilled at cutting down trees. They eat the bark and use the branches to build dams and homes called lodges in rivers, streams, and freshwater lakes near woodlands.

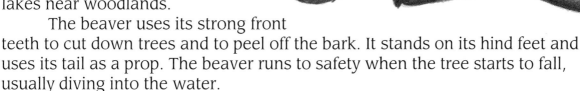

The beaver uses its strong front teeth to cut down trees and to peel off the bark. It stands on its hind feet and uses its tail as a prop. The beaver runs to safety when the tree starts to fall, usually diving into the water.

Beavers are excellent swimmers and divers. They can swim underwater for a mile and hold their breath for up to 15 minutes.

Beavers are common to North America, though they are also found in Asia and Europe.

North American beavers grow up to three or four feet long (91 to 120 centimeters), including the tail, and weigh from 40 to 95 pounds (18 to 43 kilograms). They are the second-largest rodent in the world. Unlike most other mammals, beavers keep growing throughout their lives. They live about 12 years.

The beaver uses its tail to steer when it swims. It also slaps its tail on the water to warn other beavers of danger. The beaver's enemies include bears, lynxes, otters, and wolves.

Beavers come out mostly at night to eat and work. Besides bark, beavers eat twigs, leaves, tree roots, and lily roots and sprouts.

Beavers almost always seem to be busy. Thus we call a hardworking person an "eager beaver" or say he or she is as "busy as a beaver."